In my magnificent obsession of mind over matter,
I've become the essence of the mad hatter.

excerpt from "The Obsession"
~ Jose & James

Also by Double Trouble

Double Trouble Vol I - Poems from the Edge
Double Trouble Vol II - Deviate the Levitate
Double Trouble Vol III - Poemetrics

Double Trouble Vol. IV

The Obsession

by

Matthew Jose
&
Candice James

(aka Cama Joja)

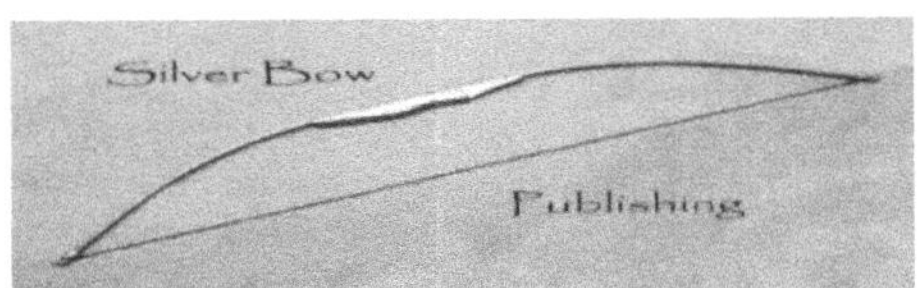

720 Sixth Street, Unit #5,
New Westminster, BC Canada
V3L3C5

3

Title: Double Trouble Vol IV -The Obsession
Authors: Matthew Jose and Candice James
Publisher: Silver Bow Publishing
Cover Art & Design: "The Pharisee and the Samaritan"
                              painting by Candice James
Layout and editing: Candice James

9781774031834 Print
9781774031841 ebook

Library and Archives Canada Cataloguing in Publication

Title: Double trouble. Vol. IV, The obsession by Matthew Jose & Candice James.
Names: Jose, Matthew, 1976- author. | James, Candice, 1948- author.
Identifiers: Canadiana (print) 2023015817X | Canadiana (ebook) 20230158226 | ISBN 9781774031834
   (softcover) | ISBN 9781774031841 (Kindle)
Classification: LCC PS3610.O75 D6952 2022 | DDC 811/.6—dc23

Dedicated to

all those fortunate
and unfortunate souls
who have lived
'The Obsession'

6

CONTENTS

8

All Kinds of Dreamers

From Harlem to Zanzibar.
From Quebec to Cairo.
There are all kinds of dreamers
and free thinkers worldwide.
They won't all be wearing garbs of distinction.
But if you pay close attention.
you can pick them out of a crowd.

Their shine will be like a brief
but sharply flickering, candle.

You might catch one leaning on a ship's railing,
pondering the plight of a long-lost Pegasus
or ruminating on the fall of Troy
at the hands of a doppelganger
claiming she is the real Helen.

You may find one carrying the dust
of an eighteen-year-old legacy of dystopian travel.
Or you may find yourself welcoming one
fresh off the frontline of crossfires and circling winds.

Then some sad morning, when you wake up
and see your life is ebbing away,
you may look into the waters of a memorial bath
and see the past parading by like a drunken clown
wearing crooked slippers and a bent smile.

You may look up at an orange melon sky
and see a time traveler beckoning to you
and you will no longer tilt at rainbows.
You will no longer ponder the breadth or depth
of Pythagorean theorems or Dempsey-like jabs
and you will turn back to the dust you were once before;
just another derelict on the loose this side of heaven.

There are all kinds of ways to prove all kinds of things
and there are all kinds of ways to put reality asunder.
But that is a seminar for another sunrise of midnight moments
and another trek through a mentally challenged mindscape
that keeps ringing in madcap songs and screaming soliloquies.

Today I will climb into a brass bowl of chickpeas
then board a banana boat bound for Panama.
In the lotus land dreams of The Professor and Sensei
I will put on mukluk slippers lined with polar bear fur
and search the empty saucers or the long-gone glaciers
until I find the keeper of the chickpea plantation,
a holly-jolly Christmas-pie soul with a toothless smile
that could melt the heart of a heartless monster
mashing the hell out of Hallowe'en terrorists.

This cinematic scene will boisterously unfold
under joyful skies and independent clusters of stars
that still refuse, after all these lost and lonely years,
to pander to or join any kind of union at all.
They are Lonestar drifters and no-account grifters
in search of a horse of a different color
and a pale stranger leading a peculiar posse.
A posse that asks no questions and answers to no one
except the Professor and Sensei.

Yes, there are all kinds of dreamers
from Harlem to Zanzibar,
from Quebec to Cairo;
and the Professor and Sensei (CaMa JoJa)
have held court and rubbed elbows
with the glorious grey matter of them all
as they dreamed a new world into being
and new beings into a brave new world.

Yes, there are all kinds of dreamers ...
And I am one who dares to dream.

Did Playwrights Really Go There?

There's a totality to the whole thing that renders it half-assed.
Alive in this state of emptiness we sometimes forget to breathe
and we're quick to forget the happy nights, aren't we?
Those nights where everybody is happy.
Everybody's laughing.
Don't ya just know it,
tonight's one of those nights
where you couldn't shed a tear to save your life.

But we just ran out of booze
and I feel a tear trying to fall tall.
So I'm going to head to the store to get more beer.
While I'm gone, I'll only be a teardrop away,
so don't fret unless you want to bust a string
in an accusatory bohemian guitar kind of way.
Put that in your meth pipe and smoke it sweet cheeks!

The heart of the matter is, it's all about the dry tears.
The kind that scrape at the lines on your face
and scratch at the holes in your soul.
I want you to put on your thinking cap and consider that
before the next distilled teardrop falls.

In the meantime, let's have a drink. I'm parched.
Of course I'm buying. That's a silly question.
I'm the type that always buys the farm,
bites the bullet, takes the dive, and always ...
always sells the waterfront property for a song.

So yeah, I'm heading to *The Pioneer* to drown my sorrows.
They stay open all night catering to the up and muckety.

I would go to the still happening old Al Capone's,
but they kicked my ass out and gave me the old 86.
Their auspicious and strawberry suspicious claim to fame
was that playwrights would stop by once in a while.

I must have gone there 8 or 10 times and never saw one.
So one night, calling the joint's bluff I yelled to the bartender,
"Where the hell are the playwrights that supposedly
drop their dollars and words and frequent this dive?"
He told me to be careful in the rapids or something like that.

And while I didn't know what that meant exactly,
I could tell it wasn't inviting or even remotely pleasant.
So I saluted him the only way I saw fit with a glass lift
a face lift and an ass lift as a parting gift, if you get my drift.

And still, after all these years, I can't help wondering ...
Did playwrights really go there?

A History of Sorts

This here is just an oral history of the thing.
Well ... actually an oral history reduced to writing.
It started as a tape recorded off the cuff discourse
that inadvertently morphed into a purple racehorse
with copious amounts of vodka trying to read the runes
laced with gin and tonic and country-western cover-tunes.

Twang is my thang at boot scootin' times like this
and honky-tonk dive bars become my muse and bliss.
So tune up that heavy Sierra pedal steel
then pick them strings 'til they spin like a wheel
and have the drummer steady on the pace
clinging tight to the beat of that Godin fretless bass.
Yeah, give it to me fast like a card sharp's ace
and rip the fuckin' freckles right off my face.

As I listen spellbound from the fringe of the thing
I know some of the words, so I begin to sing
and as I watch spellbound from the fringe of the thing
I feel like a one-trick pony in a circus ring.

So many songs but not enough singers.
So many words but no humdingers.
So many heroes and villains throughout history.
So many theories that can't resolve the mystery.

What mystery you ask as if I'm Marshall Dillon.
It's the twang and thang and the music that's still on.
It plays with my mind and unravels in my soul
every time I hear country songs or rock'n'roll.

Yeah this here is just an oral history of the thing.
Written off the cuff on a prayer and a wing.
So take my words and music and blend them in a sieve.
Hope you liked it sweet cheeks, cuz that's all I've got to give.

Dutton Dutton Dolls

A Dee Jay tress of a Dutton-Dutton doll
is in distress and threatening to fall.
And from the rear of an over-rated mall
I hear a voice and must answer to its call.

But before I do I must figure this out.
What is a Dutton-Dutton doll all about?
Is it a doll whose hair is falling out
Or a bitch at the ready to scream and shout?

And if this doll were to let fly and scream
would it be a heavy-duty type of scream machine
or would it ring like a chandelier soft in my ears?
to leave me singing through smiles and salty tears?

Daydreaming yet again ... it's what I do best

I can imagine visiting the toy factory
where these dastardly frightful little monster dolls are made.
Maybe I'd learn the secret and find the key
to what it is that makes people so scared and afraid.

My guess is that you would see a darkness of color
but even the dark would be a most vibrant shade
of fright night and fear and phobias galore.
Just the right recipe for the lost and dismayed.

I'm guessing the hallways would have mirror inlaid
and no admittance fee would need to be paid.
The tour de jour would be free of charge.
and the tour guide's name of course would be Large Marge.

These are the dreams I dream for the Dutton Dutton dolls.
I think they'd be a comfort to stallions in their stalls.
At the risk of seeming mental I really must confess
I own seven Dutton Dutton dolls and a Dee Jay tress.

But lately my Dutton Dutton dolls are running wild.
They fell under the influence of a really bad boy child.
So it looks like I'll be putting them up for adoption.
I really can't foresee any choice or other option.

The moral of this story? Don't mess with a Dee Jay tress
or Dutton Dutton dolls they'll just cause you great distress
So buy a G.I. Joe or a Ken or Barbie Doll
And run the other way if you hear the Duttons call.

The Obsession

Let the obsession take you to places beyond.
To those unknown realms you will surely recognize
as clips of forgotten film and lost photos.

They will call to you like pale ghosts resting
on the fragile cusp of pending extinction.
Erasable like a bad memory rediscovered.
Indelible like a lifetime of love gone bad.
And then over and over and over again
the broken record of missed opportunity
will play through the muted speakers
on the walls of the places playwrights used to go.
The bars and bistros they used to haunt.

In an Al Capone scenario of bullet riddled phone booths
I can still hear their voices ringing in high pitched staccato
but there's no one on the other end of the conversation.
It's pantomime city reverberating inside a desert dream
and I am the mean machine that guns down the moments
in a spray of treblified chants and altostrized rants,
shaking the foundation of the church I've inherited
in a wonderland devoid of wonder and filled with thunder.

In my magnificent obsession of mind over matter
I've become the essence of the mad hatter.
This is my measure of happiness.
This is my criterion of true madness.
This is where everyone should endeavor to be.
So let the obsession take you places beyond
until you reach the door to my den.

When you do arrive I'll be sipping a scotch and relaxing,
watching forgotten films with pale ghosts from my past
and thumbing through lost photographs ...
some I'm sure you will recognize.

Spellbound

As I watch spellbound
from the fringe of the thing
I can say with relative certainty:
the bottle never lies.
And waking each morning
is like remembering a dream
from the hinterlands of before once more.

As I watch spellbound
by the basics of the thing
I can truthfully say
I've always believed in the need
to make a distinction
between waiting and enduring.

I've been a victim of both
so I'm relatively certain
I've seen the entire transcript

So much is owed
while nothing at all is owed.

That's the line that will accompany my day today.
Why? Because I'm leaving my wallet at home
So all debts are forgiven ... today.

We're Just the Messengers

So, we started drinking and we started thinking
and suddenly there was a piano there that wasn't there before.
And there was a girl sitting there giving the ivories a twirl.
Ok, let me tell you something.
Hearing her play was like hearing something ancient
that could solve all my present problems.

I told her she sounded like that perfect tone of *'Om'*.
And that she should never stop toning.
After that I didn't say anymore.
I just listened.

So, we were still drinking.
And we started talking about duality and non-duality.
In that moment I felt like she had the blueprint
of secret ways that nobody else knows about.

Behind the scenes that's what I was thinking.
But in front of the curtain we were waxing poetic.
Then all of a sudden she hit the most off key
of all off key piano strokes anyone has ever heard.
Almost like she busted a string
and it somehow haphazardly healed itself.

.... *(sensei enters here and begins to imprint wisdom)*

Let me tell you this Professor:
There are many liquified light switches
switching off and on in my mind
as I try to resolve the many circular sides to pianos.
I have been searching longer than a lifetime
 for the coveted lost and elusive reversible key.
And, amazingly enough, that little girl's note screech
of excruciating veracity and terror exposed the reversible key
I've been searching for since music began.
Thank God for that wonderful deafening sound.

It threw the numbers scattered in my essence
into living formulas that could finally speak.
And speak to me they did
in a strange, bizarre language we both understood.

Now I am able to easily circle the sides of pianos
and side with the circles the pianos love.
Particularly the coveted circles of fives.
Now I am able to actually design and create
beautiful ultrasonic circles of sixes.

Oh...I see you've stopped drinking.
That will never do Professor.
No, no... that will never do.

But you already knew that. Didn't you?
So let's raise a glass and drink to:
        The numbers tumbling down.
        The circles and sides of pianos.
        The meaning of a drink
        and the reasons why we think.
Don't look so surprised Professor.
I never said it was gonna be easy.

Oh yeah.... and get that little girl
to play another excruciating composition.
I believe today's music needs a wake-up call
and I believe she's the one to sock it to 'em.

We're just the messengers.
She IS the message.

Cryptic? Yes!

Everything is formed in a certain way with a certain sound.
Creation, formation, information and outformation
like the beating of a Nyahbinghi drum under the calloused hand
of a devilishly devout Rasta bredren or sistren.
Yeah, I would imagine that's the sound.

But that's hardly anything.
compared to the sounds of places I've lived
and the uptown and down dirty places I've drank in.
Some of them were outlandish graffiti laden noises
accompanied by a bell ringing in a lot of trouble.
But trouble makes stories, you know?
I'll stand by that statement. In fact, I'll stand on it.

Ah, yes ... now this is beautiful.
The view from on top of this precarious perch
is a private weird zone usually occupied only by zany parrots.
From here I kind of, sort of, see that beauty is nothing
in the societally motivated blinking eye when lips are formed
just a little like that ... or a smidgeon like this.
It all looks so grabbing and gross from up here.
Wow! What a mind-boggling thirst inducing moment this is.
So I head to my favorite watering hole at a trot, then a gallop.

Pretty soon, everybody is drinking and talking,
and all the while the music's swaying
to the beat of irascible squealing tires
romping in ecstasy up and down an oil slicked street.
And that moment thunders with its own certain sound
in a truly superb style of overstated undertones
buried beneath a zillion mutant smooth, smooth stones.

Then suddenly I'm standing beside
an overly romanticized street side café image
the perfect hangout to flex the imagination's biceps.

I read a quote about something like that once.

It may have been a J.D. Salinger zinger.
The quote had something to do with natural brunettes
and Elizabeth Taylor claiming to be one.

So now I'm thinking Imma gonna go to the library
and look for a cryptic Salinger secret message
once written on an Elizabeth Taylor lock of hair
that's probably hidden in a scruffy book
that nobody wants to touch let alone read
but Imma gonna borrow it and sorrow it
with my pent-up poet tears to cleanse my mind
and then I'll crawl back into my crypt
to read and decrypt the cryptic message.
And then I'll chart out a trip-tic.
I'll head to the mall with my piggy bank.
I'll buy a new flashy pair of ill-fitting spectacles
to look like a cool blind dude, Stevie Wonder style.

So, Imma gonna bust out on a run
To the beat of a Bangkok drum
I'm gonna outrun the sun
I'll be the master thief with a gun
Move over Castor Greave .. here I come.

A pesky little Crib Tick? No
Possibly it's Cryptic? Yes.

Eat your heart out Liz Taylor
and grab another bottle of dye.
It's on the house...then on your hair

And as Jackie Gleason would say ...
Har har hardy hair hair!

So, You Write Too Huh?

So many of the words I ever wrote back then
weren't meant for anyone's eyeballs but my own.
Back then I rarely edited my stuff,
I wrote it, yeah ... but I never read it.
When I say that out loud and walk toward it out loud
I become a very slow easing creature
trapped on a dead-end street inside my I-5 psyche.

But after a bottle and a half of wine
I get a glimpse of another road up ahead.
That's when I know there is no time left
for writing about delicate things.

I'm referring more to the grungy words
and mercenary guns for hire here
that emanate from boarding houses,
hostels and seedy-side rooms for rent.

Oh, you write too? That's fantastic. It really is.
You lived in Greenwich Village at that time too?
Back then I knew I wasn't ready yet.
I hadn't lived enough, suffered enough, done enough yet.
But I wanted so badly to be a writer.
The deep-down wanting and hunger.
You gotta do it for the love of it
cuz it's tough to make a livin' as a poet.
Yeah... don't ya just know it.
Anyhoooo. Enough about me. So ... you write too huh?
Guess you got a day job too cuz your shoes are shiny
and your clothes are expensive!
You must write screenplays ... you couldn't be a poet
cuz it's obvious you ain't livin' the life man.

Blissed Out

Sometimes the whole thing doesn't feel real.
But it only lasts a few moments for me.
I'm hoping to extend those moments as time goes by.

I used to try everything I could think of to extend them.
Then one day I decided to stop trying
and that's when the moments started getting a bit longer.

Legend has it there are monks
who can stretch that state of mind into perpetuity
without turning into pieces of rock or lumps of coal.

At one with the feathered down
of the cosmic consciousness,
alive in the past, present and future of the eternal now,
they maintain a never-ending state of bliss..
They are ... *"Blissed Out"*

If I asked one of them how they were feeling
I wonder if they might reply with,
"This is the good stuff!"

Or maybe they would say,
"It's like a special kind of binaural instrumental
of the seventh and most beautiful kind."

Or they may just shrug and say,
"There's no way to explain some things.
They are simply *'the universal will'* manifesting."

I've seen the pathway to Nirvana in my dreams.
I've heard the echo of the monks' voices
whispering in the mists of the haunted Himalayas.

In my sleeping state they seem to be calling me home
but then I awake and the dream dissolves
and I'm left untethered, adrift in the real world again.

Sometimes only the sleeping state seems real
but it always gives way to the waking world.
One day I'll remain in the true moment of sleep.

In the dip and dive of entering that singularity
I will become part of the plenitude of stars
in a never-ending state of bliss ...

Kissed in on a Friday
in a highly wakened state of sleep.
Ginned up on a Saturday
inside the eternal shine of my mind.
Blissed out in the never-ending Sunday
I've been searching for all my life.

Adjustments

We are all just adjustable creatures
living in an adjustable, bustable, just a bowl world
constantly adjusting and re-adjusting to changes.

Some humans adjust effortlessly.
Some fight, kick, claw, scream and battle.
Some just simply let life happen to them.

I've seen the inside of all those movie houses:
The milk and honey love stories with no conflict.
The many-faceted horror stories afflicted and conflicted.
The lack-luster gray days that roll into one hazy fog.

Aaaahhh, sweet disappearing bird of youth fading fast,
today I am adjusting my face to fit my razor blade.
I'm adjusting my mouth to smile a bit more
and I'm adjusting my mind to be more open.

     Ad – just – ing:

Ad – I'm not taking out an ad.
Just – just because. Yeah, just because.
Ing – I'm taking it off singing-singing to be just 'Sing-Sing'.

The last one is very important requiring capitalization.
Imma talkin' 'bout Sing-Sing, the famous prison in New York
imitating the famous and as yet undiscovered prison in my mind
where I keep all my quirky, madcap incomplete poems
locked-up in layers of thick sweet air..
It's a maximum-security institution in my mind
that allows me to fit into the masses I walk with daily
in the real everyday world, where I walk as a ghost
while the rest of me flies the cosmic highway of stars.

I have learned to be an adjustable adjuster
judiciously adjudicating justified injustices.
And I have become a legend in my own mind
as the best damned adjustable adjuster this side of Jupiter.
I used Jupiter as a reference because in astrology
it is the planet of knowledge and learning.

You'll have to excuse us now
as the adjustable adjusters
have to make some minor adjustments.
The Professor has to adjust his jock strap
and Sensei has to adjust her bra strap.

So a hale and hearty ta-ta for now
from the bureau of bizarre adjustments.

Figs and Tequila and Riverbanks

I knew this poet once.
She told me, "it's easy to grow tired upon the riverbank."
But I wasn't a river-man at the time
so I didn't cotton onto the full gist of the jive talk.
But I felt the rhythm, so I got my mojo on.
and I have a better understanding now, I think.

My guess is she was talking about the length of days,
the dark of nights and the endless sad realities
of no-account nomads lost in crossroads areas
and hapless hobos traveling trains to nowhere.

Plenty of roads do in fact lead to riverbanks
or tranquil meandering rural trails.
And plenty of never-ending railroad tracks
lead to overpopulated, high-rise infested major cities.

Right when I was starting to feel forever trapped
in the bloodshot eye of a sleepy storm.
It's a calm place and all...
but you just know danger's only a heartbeat away.
Eventually it will close in on you
with the choke hold of all choke-holds.
But as for me? I was lucky in the end.
One of the crossroads decisions I made
did eventually lead me to the most majestic riverbanks.

Fast forward to another time another place

One morning I was walking the streets of Alexandria, Egypt.
I was following a lead on a fig seller
who I was told also sold tequila on the side
and I had a mean hankering for figs and tequila at the time.

When I finally tracked down the vendor,
he told me he had the figs and tequila I was looking for.
But he also said he had something much ...
much more intriguing than that to offer me.
He could take me to see the riverbanks of the Nile
from a spot no one had ever viewed them from.
He was right, I was certainly intrigued.

I asked him to take me there as soon as he could.
He motioned to nobody there and lo and behold
the most alluring and sultry Egyptian goddess
moved in on a sweet river breeze of coveted air.

I was speechless as the vendor took my money
and the goddess took my trembling but willing arm
and led me as a child, a friend and a lover
to the sacred riverbanks of the Nile.
She held my heart and my face in her silky hands
and told me she knew this poet who once said,
"It's easy to fall in love on the banks of the river
with a vibrant hobo-poet who is a river-man."

I wasn't a river-man at that moment in time
but I told her I was a true blue-blooded hobo poet.
I vowed to her right then and there, sealed with a kiss,
I'd be her hobo-poet, river-man forevermore.

Now, eternities later, we're still ecstatic together.
It's never dull or gray. It always is fair weather.
On the Nile Riverbanks, we drink tequila and eat figs
and we're joy multipliers in our wild Egyptian digs.
and as the world passes us by, like an aging wig
we dance to our own beat and don't give a fig.

Pink and Purple Maple Surple

Do I feel double-triple, super-good right now?
Nope. I feel even better than that.
To steal a phrase from the infamous Mary Poppins,
I feel super-duper, supercalifragilisticexpialidocious
I'm on a natural high babyface.
So high I can almost fly.

I am pink and purple. I am maple surple
traveling a neon night, walking through dark forests
searching for patches of moonlight
in this indigo-ink, dark, ebony sky.
When I find shiny bits of scattered moonlight
I'll sew them to the edge of night
to illuminate a sequined pathway to usher in
a wet derelict washed up grunge band
of sad, reclusive, out of touch, ne'er do wells
who left their mansion in the sky unattended
and fell to earth in a clash of cymbals and snares.

Have you ever had one of those nights?
When you knew it was a special night;
a one in a million night of nights
that somehow manages to keep repeating itself.

And then there's the constant ground hog day
disguised as a lost and found day repeating itself
on the first afternoon in a summer that simmers;
with a cow dancing to a cat with a red-hot fiddle
electrifying the atmosphere and wowing the masses
rocking and rolling an old wild-west tune
with smooth whiskey, rot-gut, cold beer and hot jazz
to the rhythm of reggae, and Basin Street blues.
It feels the same but somehow brand new and exciting.

It's super-duper, supercalifragilisticexpialidocious ...
And I am so-o-o-o pink and purple and maple surple.

Don't Ya Know?

Just the other day I was half dead
and in need of a tall cool beer, round about mid-morning.
So I threw down a get up and go to a Bistro Mexicano
Walked out of here, walked into there, ordered a beer
and ordered my favorite rice bowl
with fresh salsa, diced apple, avocado and cilantro.

The girl at the next table overheard me.
'Hey dude, don't ya know cilantro ruins everything?'

I eyed her suspiciously and slightly semi-viciously.
"No it doesn't. Some people just can't appreciate it.
But I like to put it on almost everything."

She vehemently spewed through a smile "I hate Cilantro."
But I noticed she was looking me up and down
in a rather appreciative manner.

I looked at her, 'So you really don't like cilantro?"
She screwed up her nose "That's putting it mildly.
I absolutely abhor it and hate it with a passion!"

I took a hefty pull on my beer and sighed wistfully
"Thank God for that. We'll get along just fine little girl.
Don't ya know? ... Opposites attract."

Well it was all uphill kisses and smiles from there to here
And now we're imbibing and discussing the benefits and perils
of parsley, dill, basil, and chives.
And I bet we're together for the rest of our lives.

Why?
Because opposites attract ... Don't ya know?

Drinking and Thinking

If you tip the bottom of the bottle toward the heavens
then take a really long pull, and slow back-down draw,
for a moment it's like you're sitting in a small room
with all the shades pulled down.
And just before you reach out to raise the blinds,
you think ... I've really nailed the process this time.
I'm a writer now!

I know that school of thought. Been there. Done that.
When you think you gotta drink if you wanna write,
and you gotta drink hard if you want to be a GREAT writer.
Right? Well...turns out not so much.

Some people are born to be writers, and that's great.
Some people are born to be drunks, and that's great too.
But it's the few ... so very few ... who were born to be both.
So let's recap, shall we?

You can be the greatest writer in the world
and never touch a drop of the stuff.
And you can be an illiterate drunk
who can't even hold a pen, never mind use it.
And once in a while a fusionist explosion happens
out in the cosmos somewhere.
It's usually about 1,700 years after an event like this
that a human is born on the planet some refer to as Earth.
And that human grows to be a master of both arts.
Drinking and writing. Like Hemingway, let's say.
Some say this phenomenon is a rarity
throughout the reign of humans as a dominant species.
And that's not bad considering the human reign
doesn't look like it has the longevity of dinosaurs in its genes.
So yes, drunken literary masters should be applauded.
As should the sober ones.

Drinking and thinking ... Thinking and drinking.
Such a vicious circle. Such a volatile combination!

It's so easy to get swallowed up by the liquid nightmares.

The sober ones remember the feeling behind each scar
but the drunks abstain from remembering the depth of the cut
and never feel the wounds as much.

That's worth something. Right?

Well mebbee ... mebbee not.

Eggshells

It can feel like cracking eggshells at times.
That's the whole grift, drift and gift of it.
Cracking eggshells on the bowl's lip
bruising the air that gets in the way
as the spilling contents joyously whisper:..

> *No more cages. No more shackles.*
> *No more coops or chicken cackles.*

Once the shell splits and spills its contents,
the yolky center and gelatinous outer region
start fighting for that best place space
to dominate positioning on the bowl bottom.

That's what it's like when I write the words.
The ink spills, finally freed from the pen base
and expands to take on the form of the letters.

And for some strange reason, when I'm cracking eggshells
images of Henry Miller cross my mind ... sometimes.
Now that's even stranger than strange
because I've never read a word Henry Miller wrote.
Not on purpose. I just haven't yet. But I know his name.
But I've never read a single, solitary, lovely little word
that spilled from his pen base and formed letters
before he epitaphed his way out of this world.

> *No more scribbles. No more writing*
> *No more dribbles or ink stain fighting.*

I daresay, I do say we both have a lot in common.
Both of us eccentric humanitarians in our own way.
He probably cracked eggshells and thought of others too.

Higher States of Consciousness.

What about the highest states of consciousness?

When a sculptor makes an image
it's revealed by a removal of material,
not by addition.
When a painter creates an image
It's revealed by addition of pigment to canvas or paper,
not by a removal.

There was a time
when I thought having a blank mind
was what it was all about.
   … I was wrong …
well, not all the way wrong,
just mostly wrong.

In the higher states of consciousness
paltry little things like opinions don't cut it; don't matter to me
and by analogy I could say what other people think of me
is also of little concern to me lately.
I used to care and on some lower level, I still do care,
but in a different way now.

A teacher of karma appeared before me two weeks ago;
someone I've known for eight years, mebbee more.
but only just now, hanging by a hair,
am I ready to be the student.
That's why she hadn't revealed her real self before.
Because I wasn't ready but now I am and I'm setting up my new digs
for the resurrected, reinvented me, myself and I
and my new and reborn thoughts, themselves and they,
And … get this …we're going to be
Triplitized fraternal twin students in residence.

We had to be fraternal twins. We couldn't be identical
or there'd be no room for meaningful discussions
or different points of views, cues, and news.

And how drop-dead boring would that be?
More boring than a herd of comatose turtles.

So ta-ta for now.
The fraternal twins
are each heading out to peruse and choose
their own personal preference of fraternity.

Then it's back to the proverbial drawing board
of thinks and things and thoughts and bots and dots.
And you can bet your sweet bippy we'll both be there
debating the ups and downs and pros and cons
of the higher states of consciousness and comedy
and how karma isn't always a bitch ...
sometimes it's just a dirty rotten bastard.

Yeah... sometimes that's just the way the ball bounces
or if you prefer just the way the cookie crumbles
in the higher states of consciousness.

When Luggage Speaks

I was at a flea market recently.
And I love thrifting. Since a youth
I've been learning the ways of the tag-sale-ing masters.
The bargain hunting ilk. These types are my kindred.
My sistren. My bredren. My people.

Anyway, I was at this flea market a week or two ago
and this vendor had the most incredibly magical looking,
antique, steamship, luggage set for sale.
It seemed to speak to me.
Looked like it was right out of the Titanic days.
And I've always been fascinated with those times.
And that ship. And this luggage was saying
"Buy me. Buy me and take me out of this shit-hole joint."

It was a 3-piece set. A big one, medium one and a small one.
They were all leather-bound and had a high-brow vibe to them.
Probably top-shelf when they were purchased.
They were in pristine condition. They even gleamed.
They were sharp and bright alright.
And I swear they really spoke to me.

So this guy had a price tag of 125 bucks for the set
resting on top of the middle-sized chest.
And I only had 90 measly crumpled-up bucks
in the front right pocket of my jeans.
I explained the financial situation of my denim
and he mind-chewed on that a bit and coolly said.
"The first thing you do is say yes
when a decent offer comes to the table.
Sure. Let's do 90 smackaroonies. Oh, and BTW,
got any shin plasters?" He winked. I ignored him
because I had no idea in hell what a shin plaster was.

He looked at me quizzically
so before he could ask again I paid up,
grabbed the van and pulled up
to load up my trippy luggage purchase.

They stacked super easy like Russian nesting dolls.
but as I was loading the smallest chest in the set,
something fell out of it. I scooped it up.
It was an age-old, world-worn letter of some sort
almost eerie and very foreboding,
It looked to be from the same era as the luggage.
So I opened it up and read the date February 1926.
It started with "When you read this I will be dead."

Duh...ya think so? I said to myself. What a hoot ... not.
So I closed the van's sliding door
and sat back in the front seat and continued to read.

"I'm sure we've never met, but I had to tell someone.
My name is Bartholomew Rast-Harp Putingrad.
I was a sharp bladed swordsman in Leningrad
And was commissioned by the Grand Boop Don
To kill King Louis the "in between 13th and 14th
and the Grand Boop Don would erase his name
from all forms of written history."

I sat back, lit a fag and continued to read,
"King Louis the 13½ was doomed from the start.
He had 4 legs and 6 arms and was a bitch to clothe.
He had fish-eyes, overgrown eyebrows, liver lips
and a big, humongous schnoz that just wouldn't quit;
and to boot he was one mean son of a bitch.
They whispered behind his back calling him
The human China catastrophe ... Duh and double Duh.
What the hell did they know about catastrophe.
The future China virus would make him seem
like a stroll in the park. Child's play with Chucky.

By the time I finished the amazing letter,
I was certain that history had been thwarted
and the deformed nasty, French Royal,
had really existed so I've made it my lifelong quest
to uncover any piece of evidence I can find
to prove this minor miscreant did draw breath.

But alas to no avail. I am now 96 sun revolutions old.
I have less than 24 hours to live and am deeply saddened

I have wasted my life in a fruitless hunt
looking for a malformed French king's fingerprint,
or toeprint or anything at all to prove his existence.
To prove the letter in the luggage
was speaking the truth;
but finally, after all these misspent years
I've come to terms with this one inescapable fact:

When luggage speaks ... it doesn't.
Luggage can't talk.

TV Dinners

Do you remember those TV dinners
that came in the metal tray containers?
You just had to throw them in a preheated oven
and viola, a perfectly segmented meal and no prep time.
I loved dipping into the segmented sections,
but not at a kitchen or dining room table.
We ate them on TV dinner tables and watched TV
After dinner, they were wiped clean, folded up
and hung on their TV dinner tray holding rack
until the next TV dinner episode.

I still remember our trays with affection.
They had a far-out paisley design on them.
My best friend at the time had the E.T. trays
and I was always so jealous of that.
But that's a story for another poem:
        "TV dinner tray envy."
        I'll write that one later.

Now, back to the TV dinners of yesteryear.
My mom always bought the Swanson brand.
I can still close my eyes and see the logo
in the top left-hand corner of the packaging.
The fried chicken and Salisbury steak were my faves.
I always ate every segment completely
before I delved into the coveted dessert.

        The cherry pie or cobbler.
           Or apple.
        Or oh that luscious brownie!

This one time, just for kicks, I started with dessert first.
I don't know what came over me.
I was like a kid possessed!
I got about three quarters of the way through it
before my folks even noticed.

AND then ... when they did notice, they were not happy,
but as time went by they tried *'dessert first'* too
and said with surprise, "I like it that way."
So from that day forward we deserted the first course
In favor of the *"dessert first syndrome"*
that had so innocuously overtaken our dinner protocol.

It was then that the inner me, the mini me, was born.
From that point on I mixed it up in all my endeavors,
plying, shaping and molding my inner creativity
into a super finely honed needle of imagination.

I often reflect on the old days of TV dinners
and I wonder where I'd be today without them;
without the influence they had on me.

I'd probably be bored to rat shit
and eating out of tin cans
cutting my fingers on jagged lids,
harming my human flesh and blood writing tools
to the point of interfering with the flow
from brain fog to thought to fingers to page.

I'd be a silly, willy-nilly, foo-foo frustrated writer,
or mebbee, not even a writer at all.

Egads!! Horror of all horrors!
To be a stranger to words.
Unable to express myself in vivid colors
spilling onto the stark white pull of the page.
It would be a fate worse than death.

I would be more than frustrated.
I would be marginalized;
But I'm not ...

Thank heaven for the old days
and the old ways,
and thank God for TV dinners!

Moving and Shifting

Lately I've been getting mega fed up
with smarmy, socially-sickening people.
The goody two shoe bunch just doesn't fit me anymore.
The backroom bedroom slipper crowd has exposed them
in a most personal and unflattering way:
A bunch of hole in the sole/soul, fake do-gooders.

Just the other day I found myself in a crappy situation.
I was at a 'mutual admiration society' meeting
and all the pasted- on smiles and gooey, lying compliments
almost made me up-chuck the contents of my mind.
        I wanted to *amscray astfay*
but there were no exits or escape hatches in sight
so I just kept moving and shifting about in my seat,
fidgeting with my eyelashes,
        (I left my sunglasses home)
and scratching my assaulted and peppered ears,
        (I left my bullshit extractors home too).

Now in this unfortunate moment of truth,
surrounded by this gaggle of honking, goofy geese
it's beginning to border on the unbearable.

Enough
with the *'please and thank you'* bit.
Enough
of the *'you look magnificent Scarlett'* bit
Enough
of the *'you look so handsome Rhett'* bit.
Sometimes *"enough"* is waaaay too much!

Here they strut these egomaniac bi-polar maskers
deep in thought, oblivious to their surroundings,
conjuring up the next smarmy lie they'll spin.

But maybe I'm the one missing the point,
rocking a boat that's been docked for so long.

The level of profundity regarding this thought
is moving and shifting my dormant synapses around
into different and unfamiliar electrical units,
dislocating them like WWII displaced persons.
They are lost and have to learn a new language.
And so, I sit here shifting uncomfortably in my seat.

Suddenly everything moved in a crazy fast forward spin,
twirling and whirling in a massive tsunami rewind.
Then suddenly things started to slow down.
I envisioned weekends spent in the Bahamas
and these visions helped stop all that moving and shifting
I looked around the slowly recovering room
at all the phony faces wearing masks,
changing places, spaces and faces
because they didn't like who they were.

It was an apocalyptic epiphany of megaton proportions!.
I stopped all my moving and shifting in my seat.
I stood up, stood tall, unmasked my fake date
and I walked ... no ... I ran out of that honking goose room.
Alone, in overdrive, at break-neck speed,
faster than the speed of Evidarian lumen-light.

Outside in the freshest of fresh, fresh air
I took a deep breath and realized
all that really matters is being true to yourself
and staying unmasked for all the world to see
the apocalyptic, cryptic, epiphany that's YOU!

Then the moving and shifting uncomfortably,
in the seat life has dealt you, will stop
and you will dwell in the temple
of your own ultimate seventh happiness
forever and ever, amen.

Amen brother ... Amen.

In My Mind?

In the long run I hope to remember very little of it.
I thought I might save one little ember of it.
That can lead to a forest fire of creativity,
but on second thought I decided against that.

Looking around the convention center floor,
I had no idea what everybody else was thinking,
which I found a tad quaint and most disconcerting,
as this was a conference focused on defining
and explaining the origin of thought.

Another thing that stuck with me was the theory
that the more you let go of a thing
the more you can control it.
Paradoxical to say the least.
And I had been guilty most of my life
of trying to control things
I had no business trying to control.

Like just yesterday evening.
Part of me was saying accept things as they are.
Another part was saying it's better to fluctuate.
Had I known then what I know now
I would have practiced the mindfulness technique
I learned at the conference.
The technique where you close your eyes,
practice the 5-point breathing activity for a minute or so.
and then envision you are watching a snake swim in water.
You're supposed to see how effortless and graceful it looks.
But I'm more than super-deathly afraid of snakes
so this was very uncomfortable for me to say the least.

If I chance to see them when I'm hiking
or if they slither across the lawn at home
I scream a silent mind scream, throw caution to the wind
and run a hundred clicks a minute in any direction but theirs.
Even when I see them on TV I slam my lids shut.

I'm afraid their image may indelibly imprint
on my retina and manifest at unguarded moments
and when I close my eyes to go to sleep I'll see them.
In my mind.

This mindfulness technique was unsavory indeed,
but for some inexplicable reason
when I was doing the mindfulness thing
the snake was no longer scary, not much of a threat at all.
It was as if I had faced my fear down.
In my mind.

So on my way home I stopped in at the reptile house
to prove I had conquered my fear of snakes.
Wrong move. Worst decision I ever made.
I almost pissed myself when I entered the dark
and heard that echoing sinister rattle and hiss.
.
I knew this was no baby shaking a toy.
This was a fucking snake, and I was on its hit list.
I turned tail and vamoosed at the speed of shock
before that dirty, low-down, yellow-bellied varmint
could strike and make me bite the floorboard dust,
in this shit hole of a reptile sanctuary.
And, whoever said any of them deserved sanctuary
should be shot with the balls of his own shit.

Right then and there I decided conferences suck
and vowed I'd never attend one again.

And, in total frankness, I swear to you
snakes are NOT beautiful when they swim.
Even in clear blue tropical turquoise blue waters
they are still ugly, fugly fucks!
In my mind.

The Luck

Maybe all we are is talent mixed with circumstance.
I heard that once. Can't remember where or when.
Anyhow, who, what, where or when matters not.
As time goes marching by in a bastardized two-step
to the railroad, clickety-clack of Johnny B. Goode,
Chuck Berry is still scratching his head
wondering if Johnny was the leader of a big old band
or did he just spot trains and dig songs in the sand.

I think creative talent has to boil to the surface.
It's too hot, volatile, and expansive to lay buried
in the canyons of a prodigious miner forty-niner.
There's the *Coca-Cola* "real thing" and there's the fakes.
The knock-offs, the counterfeit marauders
and no-account applauders who clap just to scratch an itch.

There seems to be an attrition quality to the whole thing,
to the duplicitous nature of the carbon copies,
and there's never any accounting for people's tastes.
Sometimes the world's greatest singer
has been relegated to and imprisoned in
his shower songs, bathroom blues
and empty home-made audience pews
where both sacred and outlandish melodies and lyrics
are born, molded, stretched, and curved
around his vocal cords to the point of strangulation.

The luck. That's all it is. Right place. Right time.
The luck. It's hit or miss. No reason. No rhyme

Bedeep, bedeep, bedeep, that's all I have kids.
No more pearls of wisdom to scatter on that matter.
Well, ok, I have one more thing to say.
Right now, as I write and as you read,
the most amazing talent is just around the corner,
undiscovered and laying under the hair follicles
of some nondescript passerby

or maybe even someone you know,
but their talent remains unknown to the world
for none to see, or hear, or read.

So I say with genuine verve, to all the artists out there:
Painters. Writers. Sculptors. Wood carvers.
And especially novice magicians.
I say with the utmost of utmost belief in these words:
Don't let lack of recognition ever define your worth!

That mind frame is a no-win mind game
and the greatest destroyer of any talent
that every manifested in a cranial cavity.

We all want to be something different.
I just could never wrap my head around
the crush of the numbers upon the earth.
So I had to narrow things down
through the lines of a poem
striving to find the key to being there
at that certain spot, at that certain time,
on that destined dot, on that destined line.

That's the luck. That's the chance card.
Some are holding a loaded deck
but all I'm holding is this pen,
and this paper.

And, it has to be enough.
It has to be, and ... it is ...
enough.

On the Rails with Strange Red

I parked the thing in the first parking garage I could find
and had another drink.
A hankering for a drink can be as troubling
as a doorbell's incessant ringing.
So you answer the damn bell if you can.
I cracked the cap and answered the call.

I'm not apologizing or making excuses for this behavior.
I'm just saying I was living unrehearsed in those days,
and looking for something good
but instead always found the opposite.

On a good day
I was one of the four guys unloading a boxcar.
On a bad day
I was some young bum hopping on and off freight cars.
It's on a freight jump that I met Strange Red.
That was his rail name anyway.
Never did know his natal name.

He always talked about drug stores and movie houses.
If we got to a town that didn't have both he would always say,
"hey man, this ain't right! This is some screwed up piece of dirt."
And when passersby would raise an eyebrow or two
in our general direction Red would sigh and say,
"Sadly, these aren't the beautiful people we are."
But the cool thing is he would never talk too much about it.
Just enough for a point to be taken away
by anyone listening and interested.

Some search for years and never find what they seek,
but Strange Red was the type who was never searching.
He wasn't looking for anything at all,
but he sure was living more than most.
Life was always pretty much automatic to him
and that's a rarity in this world of think, think, think.

One time, we were in Texas just sitting on a park bench.
Passersby probably thought, *'what a pitiful pair'.*
But we didn't give a crap what they thought.
We were proud to be the Park Bench Boys.
There's something strangely noble and satisfying
in being one of the least recognized.

Strange, but Red could always find something to laugh at
even when we were down to our last bean; starving.
Then, when he started to feel like he was boxed in
he would jump up like pogo stick, head down to the tracks
and jump into the best graffitied box-car rolling.
He'd shadow box his way through the noisy night
until he woke up either a winner or loser.
He didn't care. Come see, come saw. No blame.
To him, the fight was all that mattered; not the fame.

Ahhh, but that was donkey's years ago
And there's no one to pin the tail on now.

Those days on the rails are gone and so is Strange Red.
I'm a city slicker now, and least what I seem to most I know.
How I'd love to be back on those rails with Red
instead of here on these rails I'm careening off of,

Maybe if he were here he'd find something we could laugh at.
But he's not here ...and I'm out of control
on the rails of my own making ...

And nothing's funny anymore.

Time Passes Until It Doesn't

I am grateful for the passage of time usually,
but I can't ignore the weight of time passing.
Can't turn a deaf ear to its heavy footsteps
or ignore the obvious existential questions it poses.
I dwell on them daily. Questions that won't quit,
Questions like: Why can't I just be grateful with time passing
and be aware of my imminent death simultaneously?
They don't have to be mutually exclusive, do they?
But, then again, could they really be mutually exclusive,
or just two abstracts circling in mutual reception.

A rhetorical echo bounces like a ball in my mind.
"What is a passage really?"
Is it predominantly a verb or a noun?
In the abstract it's a verb: ethereal movement.
In the concrete it's a noun: a trail, a path.

To me it will always be verbage and abstraction.
The bottoms of valleys and the tops of mountains
all feel so different, but they're tied together
with the winding string of a nounal pathway;
a passage traveling from bottom to top
and then back down again while, on another level,
the movement of the verbage continues unbroken..

I can now see that things we don't understand
we must learn to accept as exponential unknowns;
formulas we'll never be able to solve or re-quotient
and that's fine. I can live with that puzzle.
I can rest easy knowing the missing piece
is out there somewhere for someone to find
and it probably won't be me. And that's okay too.
Hell, I didn't even know there was a puzzle
let alone a missing piece.

All I know is this. Time passes
until it doesn't ... I call that death.

The Rain Pelted

It's like when the rain begins to pelt down
and all you want to do is go to the bar
and slug a few bottles to ease the pain of the rain.
You're not worried about the money for the rent.
That's always an afterthought.
Like how a spider goes on spinning its web
on automatic, without even thinking about it,
Or like when you pen something immortal
but after you write it you lose interest in it and toss it.
And those scribbles on the empty sides of the newspaper.
Nobody ever saw those. Or read those.
And I certainly don't remember what they said,
but I have a feeling they may have been immortal.
That's how I felt at the time anyway.

I just accepted whatever happened to me in those days.
Some nights I'd drop anchor and get drunk in my room.
Just wanting to be left alone in my sea of alcohol.
But I would always bring books to my boat-bed
and I read those books with a fevered fervor:
those life-jackets kept me from drowning.
And when the rain really pelted,
I hardly noticed the droplets
and I never heard them falling at all,
but I was always aware, that everywhere,
the rain pelted harder on wet bones like me.

Today I'm just another dry bone
trying to stay afloat and dry in world of wet
stacking my skeleton with blood, sweat and tears
to keep the tsunami, just around the corner, at bay.

And all the while I remember what it was like
when the rain really pelted in those days.
I wear the invisible, tarnished bottlecap ...
Lest I forget.

Eerily Similar

Generally speaking, most of the things
the "in" people create and do have no steam in them.
No bat in the hat and things like that:
No fire. Not even a scanty leftover ember
to burn a rage or spurn a page. (poems excluded)
Ah yes, the "in" people who are really "out of it".
The lightweights that flit and fly in and out
of our lives like nondescript dandelion fluff in the wind.
And the great pretenders to the tower of intellect.
The speed scanners of heavy-duty poetry books
that babble on in their own private Babylon
where nothing really matters to their paper hearts.
I think all of them come to the stage here
at one time or another; sometimes with their brother's mother,
but once in a while someone arrives high- stepping in style
dressed in a pink plaid blazer as sharp as a razor.
At worst, a Kandinsky or Picasso mess.
Eerily similar to the best of the rest.

I want to stand tall before it all
I want to know what the bat in the hat is thinking
I want to meet that person in the pink plaid blazer.
I want to babble on in Babylon in tongues.
I want to climb ladders that have no rungs
To the gates of heaven at 10:11.

I want to pull that bat out of the hat
and see if there's a rabbit hiding in there somewhere.
I'm always trying to find what isn't there.
But, everything is there, just out of sight,
like all the colors in white.
Eerily similar to 'Lullaby and goodnight
with roses bedight' ...
echoes of yesterday tucked inside today

Some days fall into the eerily similar
horizontal clutch of the pale perpendicular.

Curious Yellow

Anxious to chart their growth as they matured,
I made sure to measure the corn stalks once a week
I recorded their upward mobility in a yellow notebook.
Not because I thought the ending heights
would be a main factor in the overall flavor profile.
I was just ... wait for it *'curious yellow'*
as to how fast and splendidly corn could grow.
I'd seen full grown stalks plenty of times before,
but never witnessed the process from seed to soil,
to table to stomach as it were.

You're probably wondering
where this whole twisted corn growing tale began.
What's the origin of this tall stalk story?
Is that what you asking yourself?
Or are you just sitting there yawning.... *'boring'*... ?
Well that's no never mind to me.
Imma gonna spit out the whole uncut saga anyway.
So, buckle up baby and get ready for
the far-out flight of fancy to Mango Grove.

I was at the grocery store a couple Wednesday's ago,
standing in the produce section, lazily watching
a store employee stock fruits and veggies on the shelves
for customers to purchase and eventually consume.
I was listlessly busy minding my own business,
reaching out from my dreamland and grabbing a mango
when an electric type of shock ran up my right arm.
The arm and hand I was grabbing the mango with.
But the shock I was feeling didn't hurt exactly.
It was intense in sensation but not painful.
Such and odd yet somehow enjoyable feeling, I thought.
And suddenly a movie started playing in my mind.
Right there as I stood in between the plantains and papayas.
Time stood there with me, and it stood absolutely still.
Mango in hand, frozen in a movie daydream,
I began to see the life of that mango

in vivid high-res color and glorious detail,
from seed to soil to produce store to my hand.
I saw it being tended to on a farm in Bermuda.
And I saw the weather patterns that manifested
throughout the course of its ripening journey.
I saw the farmers and I saw the field hands.
They were sitting and basking lazily on their breaks
under the tree they were tending to at the time
and breaking out their little lunch pails and thermos'
in the shade underneath their fruit-stained ladders.
I could even see what they were eating
as they tended to this mango now in my hand.

I put the mango down and the movie stopped.
I picked it up and the movie continued.
I thought I might be losing my mind and panicked
until I glanced at the little guy on my right
who was doing the same thing as I was ...
Picking the mango up and putting it back down
a bunch of times with a puzzled look on his face.

This whole scenario made me forget about corn stalks.
Made me think twice and realize that fruit talks,
but not in a language we can understand.
So sensing this with their enhanced intelligence
they simplify and reduce the inter-species communication
to pictures and films, colors, and smells.

These savvy non-humans that grow on earth are very smart.
Way smarter and inventive than we are.
We can't send our thoughts in words and films to them ...
Or ... can we? I guess we'll never really know
unless and until we can actually figure out a way
we can speak vocally with them
in a language we can both understand.
But that's another poem for another time.
For now I'll just have to be satisfied
enjoying the cycle of seed to soil, table to stomach
and all the while I shall remain ... wait for it ...
"curious yellow"!

The Death of One Lucky Bastard

Whenever I'd walk into my fave watering hole, they'd say
"Hey...here comes the horseshoe ...how ya doin' Lucky?"
Because they thought I had a made in the shade kind of life.
Brambles (my partner in pints and shot lifting)
said to me one sun-streaked lazy day,
"I swear someone lodged a four-leaf clover up your ass
at some point, you lucky bastard!

And on another note,
Whenever I'd walk into the drop in art afternoons, they'd say
"Hey ... here comes death ... how ya doin' death?"
Because I was very often talking about death.
Mimi (my partner in 'Purple Flame' Art)
said to me one prodigious, star-favored day,
"Why are you always talking about death?"
I replied in my usual casual manner,
"Because I'm getting to know it before I meet it.
It's who you know, not what you know."
I guess some people listen to me and think
I'm a morose, death obsessed weirdo but I'm not.
There's a method to my madness most can't see"
But that's beside the point. The point is we are all going to die
so better to shake hands with death now
and make friends with him ahead of time
so we've got an *"in"* when it's "our time to choke".

Every one of us has to stumble and fall
and unwillingly enter when we hear death call.
But I will enter unencumbered and willingly,
and death, my long-lost buddy, my friend
will come to me with open arms
and say, amidst the bells and whistles,
"Welcome home you lucky bastard.
You'll be feathered but won't be tarred ...
We're in need of a far-out visionary bard.
and you, dear bard, are one lucky bastard!"

Hankerings Increase and Decrease

Have you ever had a random hankering
early in the morning or late at night?
It can feel more important than truth.
Sometimes I wonder why I even pose these things.
But if even one person knows what I'm talking about,
then I feel I've done the world a solid.

On a completely other note, just the other day
the barista at my coffeehouse hang-out
handed me my double espresso, and said,
"Did you know that gravity increases with mass,
and decreases with increasing distance between objects?"
All I could muster for a response was a feeble,
'I haven't considered that in some time, if ever."
And the rest of the day that's all I could think about.

I tried to corollate this to the time
I saw a lady swallow a martini, olive and all,
right down the gullet quite bloody effortlessly.
You could have colored me red, blue and tattooed
and equally shocked and impressed that night.

Just last night I was seriously thirsty. I mean, parched man,
and this bottle of absinthe appeared out of nowhere.
It's rare that someone would knock unannounced like that.
in this neighborhood anyway. I opened the door
to see Vincent Van Gogh and Oscar Wilde
standing there with a bottle of wormwood for us all to share.

So ... since I had these great minds in my presence,
I asked them about the gravity of color to writing.
The weight of paint to ink and the relativity of canvas to paper.
The conundrum of passing thought to heavy thinking
and last but not least, the true indicative active
of the viscosity of the absence of absinthe.

Oscar took out his notebook

Vincent took out his portable paint kit.
Oscar then proceeded to take a big hit of absinthe
then turned to Vincent with a smirk and said,
"Vincent, dear boy, could you lend me your ear?"
Oscar was speaking figuratively but Vincent took umbrage,
stood up, grabbed Oscars' pens and pencils
and in a fit of absinthe anger broke them into pieces.

Oscar took offense and spilled Vincent's paints on the floor
Vincent took a fence (a thick picket one, no less)
and started swinging it threateningly in the air
and yelling "Oscar you're a fuckin' creep,
and your writing is utter shit...
and your latest work is a goddamned hot steaming turd.
The fight continued but I didn't give a shit.
The absinthe was all mine, so I slugged it back like a trooper.
A super-duper, trooper before I passed out.

When I awoke a few hours later
the atmosphere had changed radically
Vincent and Oscar were debating informational reciprocals
about the true nature of starry, starry nights
in relation to the actual profundity of "De Profundis.

I wasn't much interested in their social intercourse
so I grabbed my mind and my jacket
and headed to my coffeehouse hang-out
for some hot steamy liquid and words of wisdom
from the ever-erudite bistro fashionista
about how gravity increases with mass,
and decreases with increasing distance between objects."
I wasn't really much interested in that conversation
so I sat back, closed my eyes
and wondered what Oscar and Vincent were doing
and then I began to really wonder
if they were wondering what I was doing.

It truly was a revelatory revelation,
a momentous moment of wonderment
that, in the end, signified nothing.

5 Minutes

I placed the food on the table. and walked back to the kitchen
I grabbed a French Cabernet Sauvignon and a Pino Noir
Luckily, I had just watched the movie 'Sideways' the week before.
For the twelfth time. Approx.

I could hear the horn intro of Burning Spear's song
"Happy Day" playing in the dining room..
I like that song, so I hustled myself there, wine in hands.
I got there right before the first chorus started chanting.
"I just keep winning" is what I was thinking to myself.
But to my surprise, *she was gone.*

I had only been in the kitchen for 5 minutes.
What could have happened in 5 minutes?
Then I thought about all the things
that can happen in 5 minutes.
So many things, can happen in 5 minutes or less.
It takes about a minute for bomb dropped from a plane
to hit the ground. That's a lot less than 5 minutes
and it will change the course of many lives in that short time.
I couldn't shake the thought of what it must be like
to live in a God forsaken and war-torn country.
I stood at that empty table for about 5 minutes
feeling deep sympathy for those poor souls
within the blast radius...and beyond.

Then in an instant my attention snapped back
to the table hosting 2 plates.2 glasses.2 sets of silverware.
I had broken out the nice cutlery for the evening.
The knives, forks and spoons housed in a wooden box
my grandmother gave me when I was 7 years old.
Yes, I too thought it was weird she gave it to me at that age.
You're not alone. But that's a story for another day.

Right now the main feature is:
2 place settings and 2 glasses of wine.
But now ... the surprise ending. Only 1 person.

Slug Coins and Bug Doyn Carts

I wasn't sure what to do with them.
I had all these slug coins from back in the jukebox days.
I don't think I ever paid for a song back then.
Now everything's electronic, digital, all that jazz.
These slugs seemed useless in today's tech culture.
But I didn't want to just throw them out.
They had meant something once.

I figured if I threw them in the bathtub and shone them up
maybe they'd become part of a new age art project
using old days' slugs. Yeah I'll call it Slug Coin art.
I just realized I always wanted to be an artist,

Ah just another pipe dream ... gone up in smoke
Even before it grew legs to walk and lips to talk.
This Slug Coin art idea was just a token thought
I started thinking a about shopping cart screwdrivers and realized
a Bug Doyn Cart's what I really needed to fix my broken cot
It's been hell tryin' to get a decent night's sleep on that cot.
I'm so tired all the time and drownin' in the deep.
I'm gonna play "The Lion Sleeps Tonight" as a lullaby
and then maybe one of the Tokens will be a good guy
And he'll slug the hell out of the sleep robber
Yessiree mucker. Yesirree. Yessiree bobber.

Fast forward 48 hours.
I'm ready to take on the world again fearlessly
with a token to get back where I used to be.
Oh yeah, and that Slug Coin art thingie
bit the dust like a-mad dog-bitten flea.

My cot's all fixed up and I've straightened my knee.
Again they're callin' me Slugger McGee
We're happy at last Bug Doyn cart, cot and me.
sleeping effortlessly and peacefully.
dreaming jukebox dreams of musical arts
and brand-new slug coins and blue Bug Doyn carts.

Idioms for Idiots

There are things you have to find out for yourself.
I could go on for days about things,
but how on earth would that help you?
Some things in life have to be experienced
for the wisdom to be gained.

Consider these idioms for instance.
"Early to bed and early to rise
makes a man healthy, wealthy and wise."
Or does it? Maybe it's like this:
"Early to bed and early to rise
and your girl goes out with other guys."

How about this one?
When 7 white doves are released into an instant sunlight,
are they charged with excitement of just flying blind?
When they come out of the clouds simultaneously,
do they do this of their own accord
or are they being directed by a smart cloud?

And what about this one?
"Absence makes the heart grow fonder"?
Or should it be "Absence makes the heart go yonder"?
This is also something that has to be experienced.
And it is experienced differently by different lovers.
It's the credo of love: A random crap shoot.
Some gotta win. Some gotta lose.
Harry's on a high; good time Charlie's got the blues.

Here's another one to chew on.
What is the origin and meaning of "let's get down to brass tacks"?
Is it getting down to the nitty gritty essentials?
Or is it just an old slang cockney saying?
Or you could say screw it, blue it and tattoo it.
I bet'cha don't know the true origin or meaning of that.
Very few do ... but I do, and I feel it is my duty

to tell you the younger generation the real facts about it.
And believe me you can't get the real truth by googling it.

In truth, it referred to an old malady that plagued
male travelers: the armed services the merchant marines etc.
It referred to a disease they were deigned to have contracted
from dalliances and intercourse with "ladies of the night"

The old idiom, screwed, blued, and tattooed, meant:
a disease, a potential cure, and a registration number.
Getting down to brass tacks it meant.
You've got syphilis you poor bastard.
Take this blue pill or blue ointment to try to cure it,
It's a pretty good bet it probably won't cure it
so we'll tattoo your penis, so you'll be a marked man
to warn all future partners that you have or had syphilis.
When all three of the steps had been taken,
the unlucky bastard was "screwed, blued and tattooed.

You won't find that in any of your internet searches.
So much has been lost in translation through the years
and most of the screwed, blued and tattoo-ees
have long since succumbed to their syphilitic lesions.
They walk this earth no more and screw no more ...
Dead as a door nail. Or, as Dickens would say,
"Dead as a coffin nail" ... but either way, dead!.

Idioms, shmidioms. Idiots, shmidiots.
One in the same. Same in the one.
So much for idioms for idiots or to be politically correct
I should say so much for the poor unenlightened souls
traversing this dimension with little or no understanding.

But anyone who knows me
knows I never have been known for my tact.
And political correctness? You guessed it. I have none.
I was long ago dispossessed of it.

Hence the title of this poem ...
"Idioms for idiots."

Way Too Blessed To Be Stressed

We're both way too blessed to ever be stressed.
We'll keep walkin' that line and all will be fine.
Dumpin' the pressures and the work loads off.
It's Like gettin' rid of a nagging cough.

But we wouldn't have it any other way.
In a way our work is a little bit like play.
Doin' for ourselves and doin' for others
and doin' for some sistas, brothas, and mothas.

It's a makin' a name, groovin' speakin' game.
Shoutin' it out tryin' to grab a little fame
and then sooner than later it's almost all over
then we'll be residin' 'neath the grass and clover.

But you and I can say it's been a special ride
With the best of ups and downs that can't be denied
When it comes to poetry we're both over obsessed
But thanks to God who made us too blessed to be stressed.

To take a load off if you're carryin' one.
Loosen up you laces and come undone.
Here's a quick postscript of 3 syllable rhymes
so dig into your pocket for a handful of dimes

                LOL
             pell go mell
             stella fell
             in the well
             what the hell
             ring the bell
             crack the shell
             we won't tell

Thanks for lettin' us in awhile to be your goofy guest.
We unzipped our secrets and came to you undressed.
We hope you liked the gusto, the crazy and the zest.

It may not be the best
but we hope you're just a tiny, wee bit impressed.

But if not, it don't matter.
We're madder than a mad hatter
and ...
we're just way to blessed
to ever be stressed.

Author Profile:

Matthew Jose and Candice James are known as one entity, "CAMA JOJA", on their home planet Evidaris. When transporting to the Earth realm they automatically split into two entities which allows them to have separate and unusual, quirky and far out happenings which they funnel into their collaborative poe-stories which meld together the thoughts and short visualizations of Evidarian/Earthling potential and probable happenstances.